For Anaé and Jean.
Matthieu

For Flavie and her imaginary friends.
Michaël

First American edition published in 2013 by Gecko Press USA, an imprint of Gecko Press Ltd

A catalog record for this book is available from the US Library of Congress
Distributed in the United States and Canada by Lerner Publishing Group, Inc.
241 First Avenue North, Minneapolis, MN 55401 USA
www.lernerbooks.com

This edition first published in 2012 by Gecko Press
PO Box 9335, Marion Square, Wellington 6141, New Zealand
info@geckopress.com

Original title: Un mammouth dans le frigo
Text by Michael Escoffier and illustrations by Matthieu Maudet
© 2011 l'école des loisirs, Paris
Translation © Gecko Press 2012

Translated by Linda Burgess
Typesetting by Luke Kelly, New Zealand
Printed by Everbest, China

ISBN hardback (US edition): 978-1-877579-50-9

For more curiously good books, visit www.geckopress.com

A Mammoth in the Fridge

by Michaël Escoffier
and illustrated by Matthieu Maudet

GECKO PRESS

"Dad! Dad!
There's a mammoth in the fridge!"

"Don't be silly, Noah.
Come and eat your fries."

"Sweetheart—call the fire department."

Wheee-ooo! Wheee-ooo! Wheee-ooo! Wheee-ooo! Wheee-ooo! Wheee-ooo

Wheee-ooo! Wheee-ooo! Wheee-ooo! Wheee-ooo! Wheee-ooo! Wheee-ooo!

"Morning, ma'am. We're here for the mammoth."
"Oh, please come in..."

"Okay, are you ready?
One...
two..."

"Whooooops!"

Clip! Clop!

Clip! Clop!

Clip! Clop!

"Well, what now?"
"Be patient. It'll have to come down eventually."

"Huh! We could be here till fall."

"Sorry, guys. We've got to go."

"Come on. It's not our problem."

"Here,
kitty, kitty!"

"Look at these yummy carrots."

"Come on…"

"Ssshh! Don't wake Mom and Dad."

"I'm warning you—this is the last time I'll save you.
You'll get us all in trouble with your silly nonsense..."